Try a Little Kindness

HENRY COLE

SCHOLASTIC PRESS | NEW YORK

To MVMC who always said:
"Is it true, is it kind, is it helpful?"-HC

Library of Congress Cataloging-in-Publication Data available
ISBN 978-1-338-25641-3

10 9 8 7 6 5 4 3 2 1   18 19 20 21 22

Printed in China   62
First edition, October 2018

Henry Cole's art was created with pen & ink and watercolor on Bristol paper.
Book design by Christine Kettner

Now that's a hug.

A smile to greet the morning.
A hug to greet each day.
A "thank you" and a "yes, please"
Are things that you should say.

Our animal friends will show you
Exactly how it's done.
Make it a daily habit ...
Kindness can be fun!

Wake up with a smile!

Rise and shine.
Breakfast time!

Be the last in line.

Invite someone over to play with you.

Share your toy.

You'll feel so special inside.
Try some kindness every day,
A smile, a joke, or something else.
Come on, don't you want to play?

Tell someone they are special!

Be a great ally.

Write a poem for someone.

Praise someone's work!

Hold the door for a friend.

Give someone your seat.

Pick up the trash.

Visit someone who is lonely.

I know you think we did it
But our job is not quite done.
We need to keep on going.
Being kind is so much fun.

Help someone without being asked.

Read to your friends.

Write thank-you notes!

Do something unexpected.

Take a selfie with friends.

When evening has come,
And it's time to go to bed,
You brush your teeth
And wash your feet
And make sure your fish is fed.

Think of new good deeds to do,
And some nice things to say.
Then you'll know why kindness counts,
And look forward to each day.

ZZZZZZZ_{zz}